MARVEL
BLACK PANTHER

By Frank Berrios
Illustrated by Patrick Spaziante

 A GOLDEN BOOK • NEW YORK

© 2018 MARVEL marvelkids.com

All rights reserved. Published in the United States by Golden Books, an imprint of Random House
Children's Books, a division of Penguin Random House LLC, 1745 Broadway, New York, NY 10019, and in Canada
by Penguin Random House Canada Limited, Toronto. Golden Books, A Golden Book, A Little Golden Book,
the G colophon, and the distinctive gold spine are registered trademarks of Penguin Random House LLC.
rhcbooks.com
ISBN 978-1-5247-6388-6 (trade) — ISBN 978-1-5247-6389-3 (ebook)
Printed in the United States of America
20 19 18 17 16 15 14 13 12

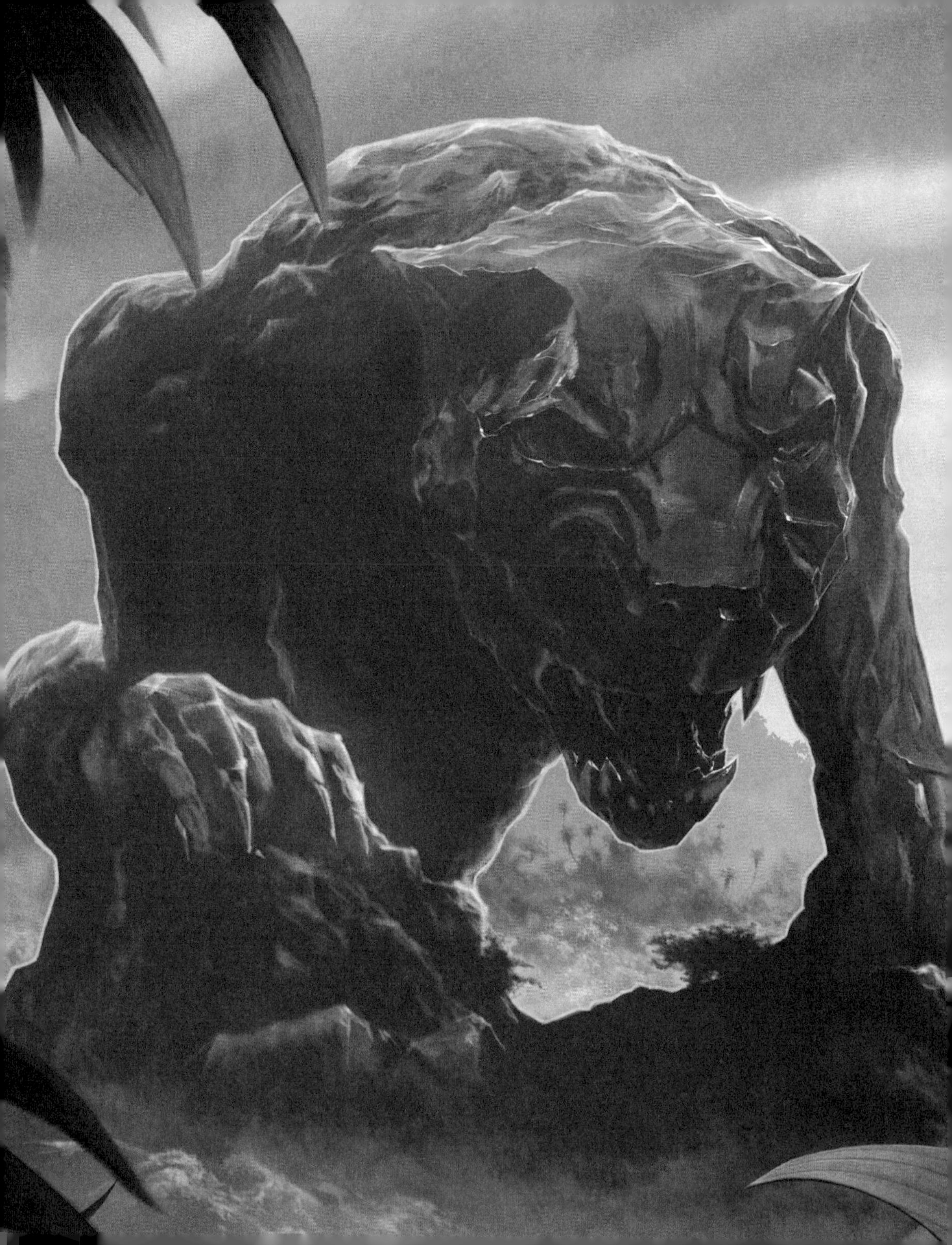

His name is T'Challa. Like his father before him, he is the leader of Wakanda, a majestic and mysterious country in Africa. But he is better known as the Super Hero called **BLACK PANTHER**!

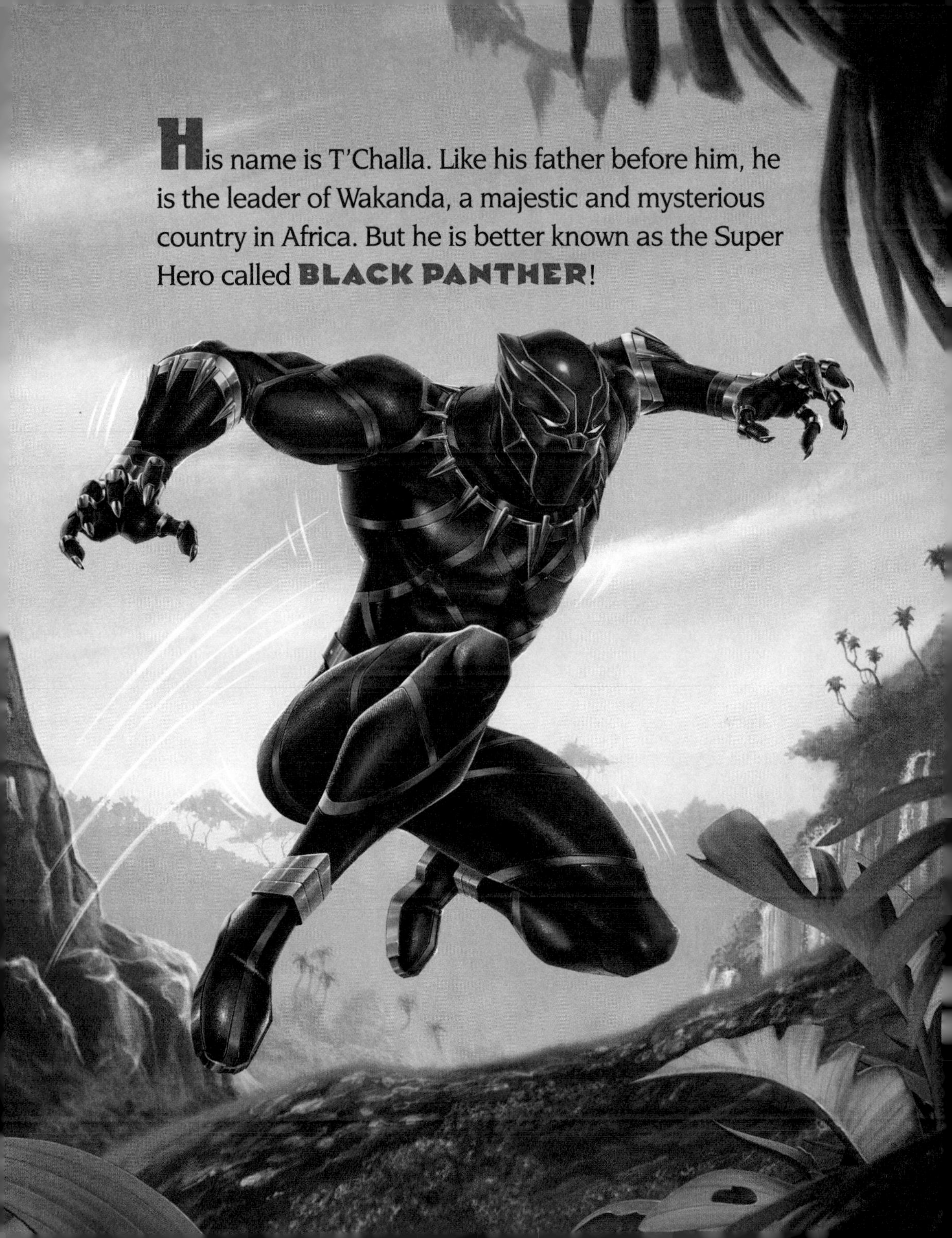

As chief of the Panther Tribe, Black Panther must use his strength, speed, and other powers to protect his people.

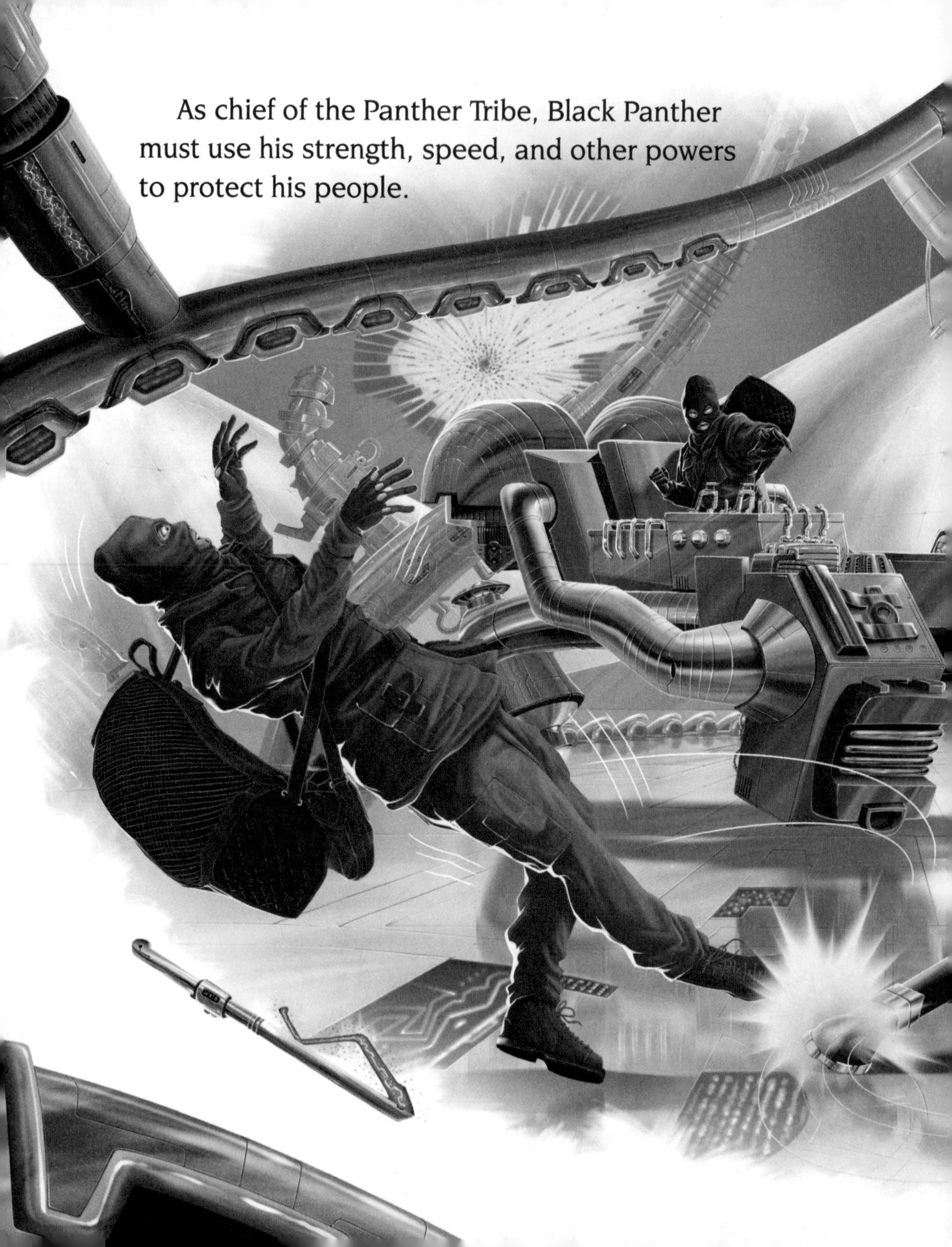

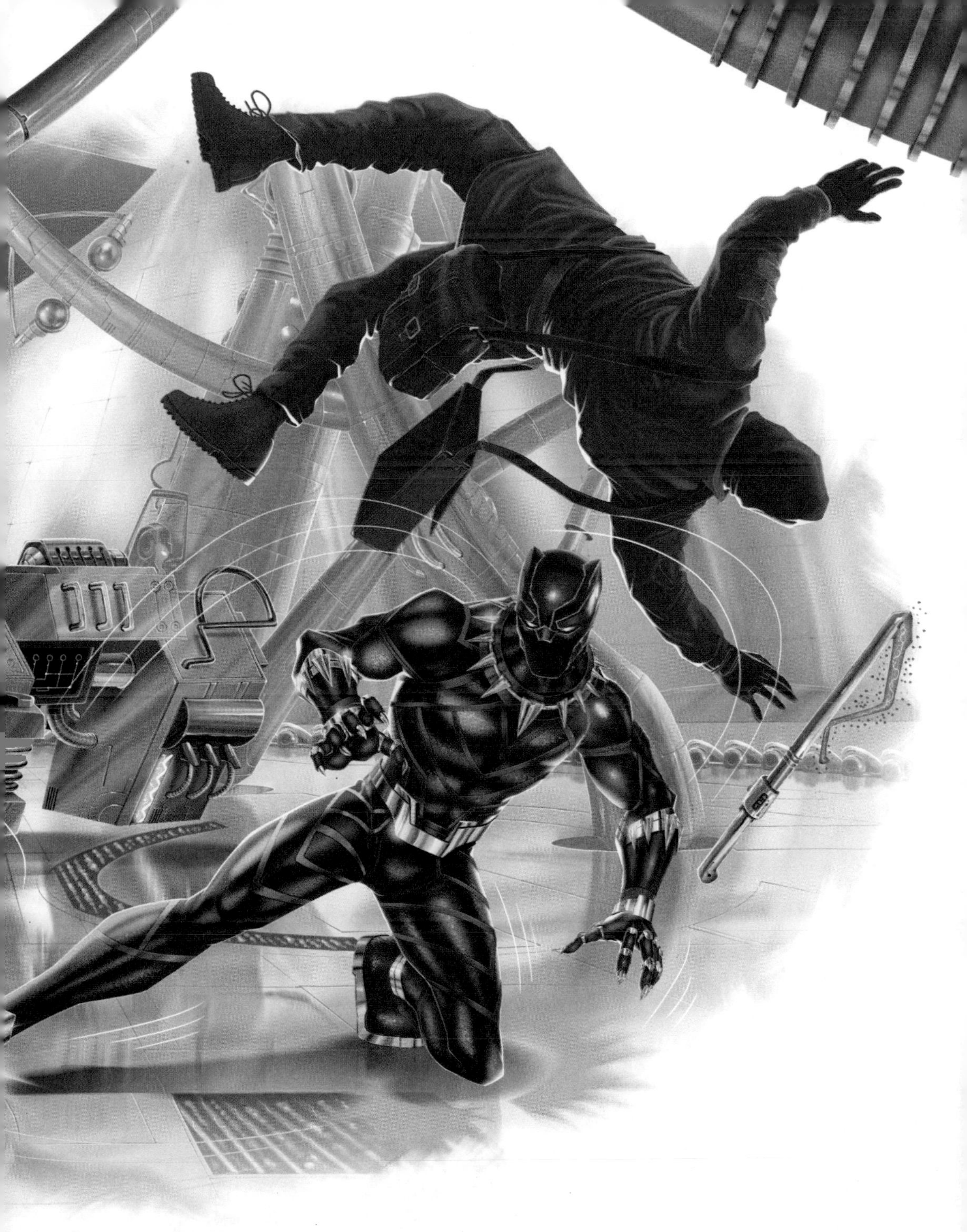

Black Panther's costume is laced with a powerful metal called **VIBRANIUM**, which allows him to absorb potent punches and deliver crushing blows!

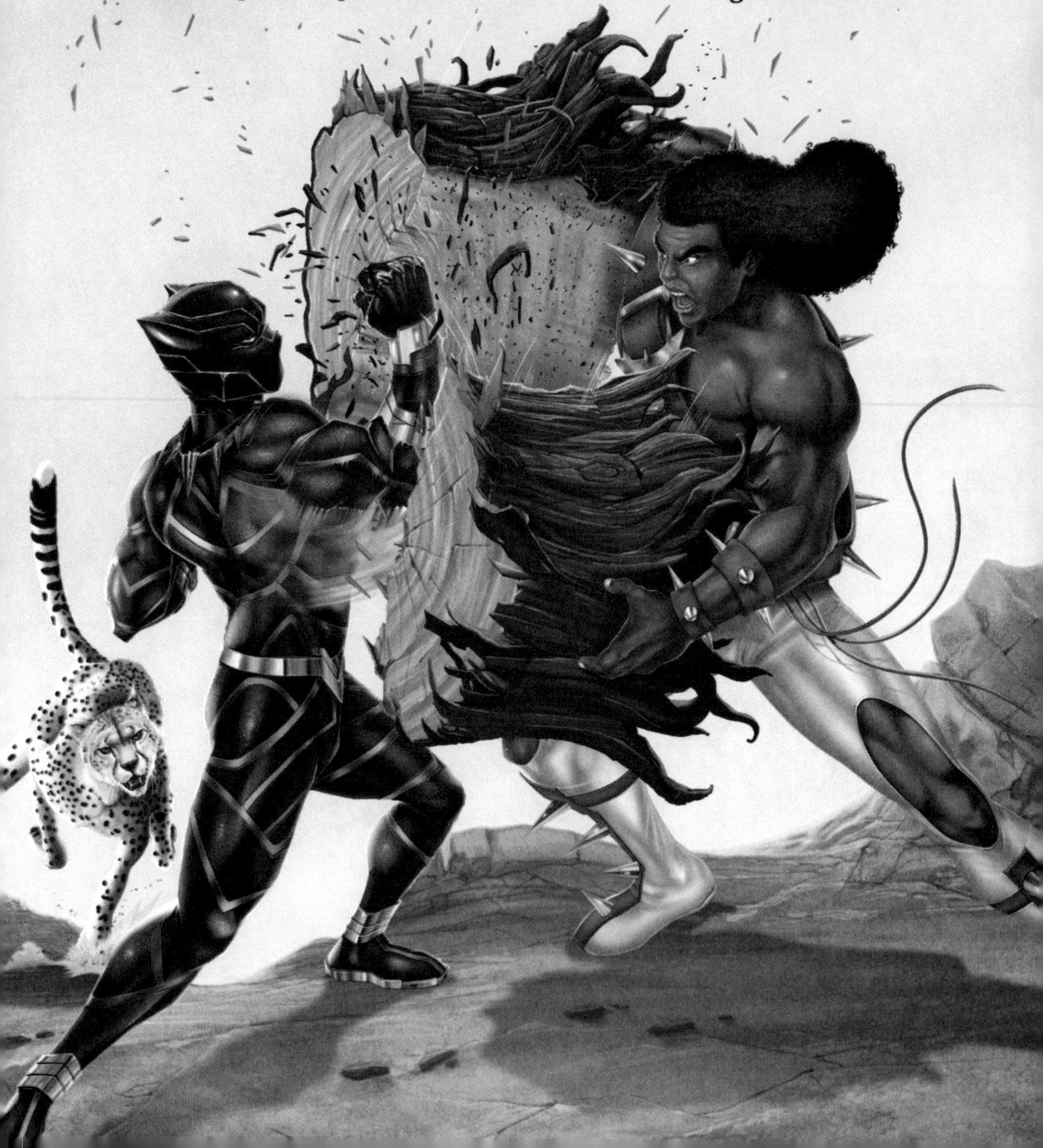

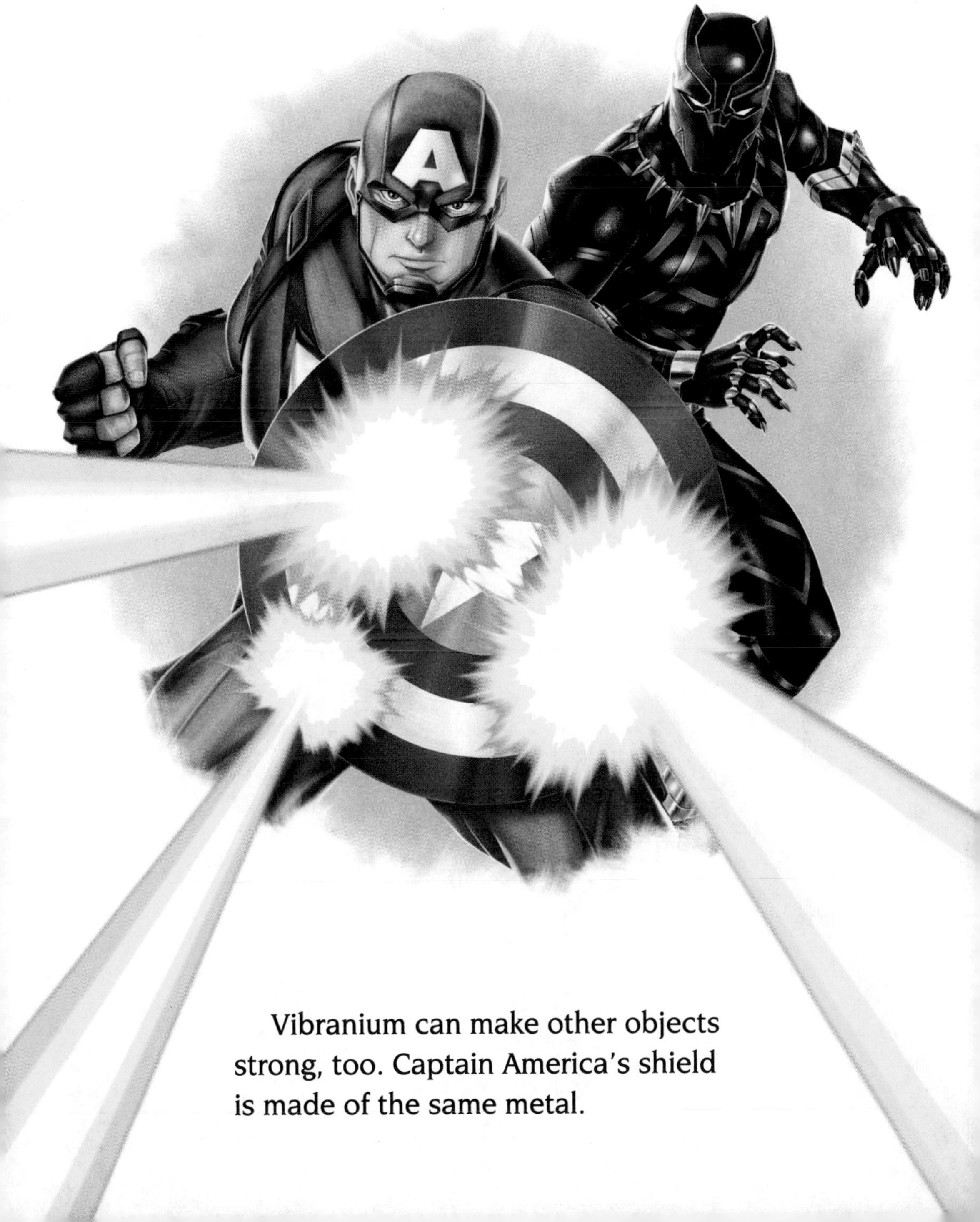

Vibranium can make other objects strong, too. Captain America's shield is made of the same metal.

The *claws* in Black Panther's costume can rip even the hardest steel!

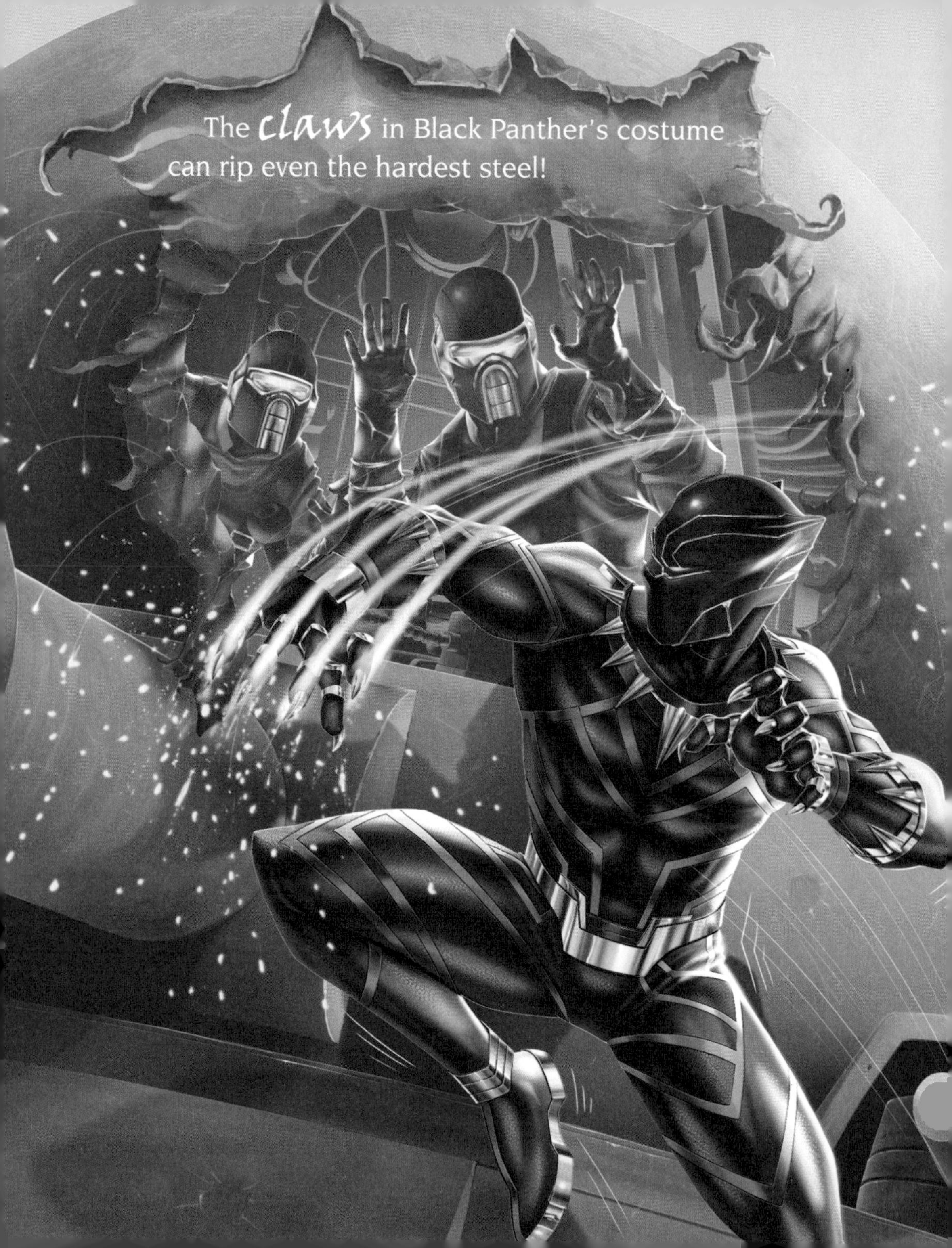

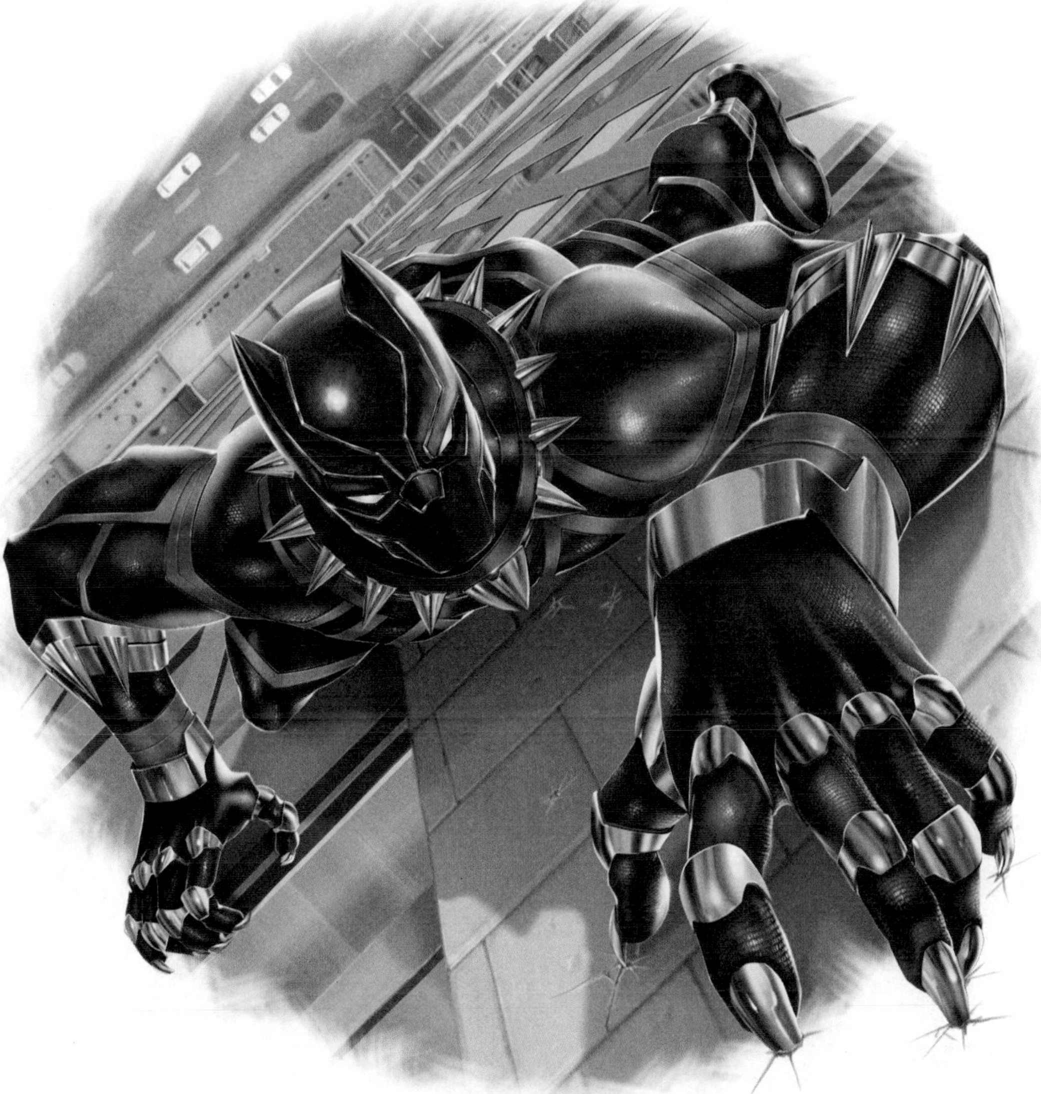

Along with his strength and speed, Black Panther uses his Vibranium claws to climb up walls and keep his balance at great heights!

Wakanda is the only place on earth where Vibranium exists. Lots of people want to steal it, so it's Black Panther's job to stop them.

An evil scientist named Ulysses Klaue was so determined to get a piece of the powerful metal . . .

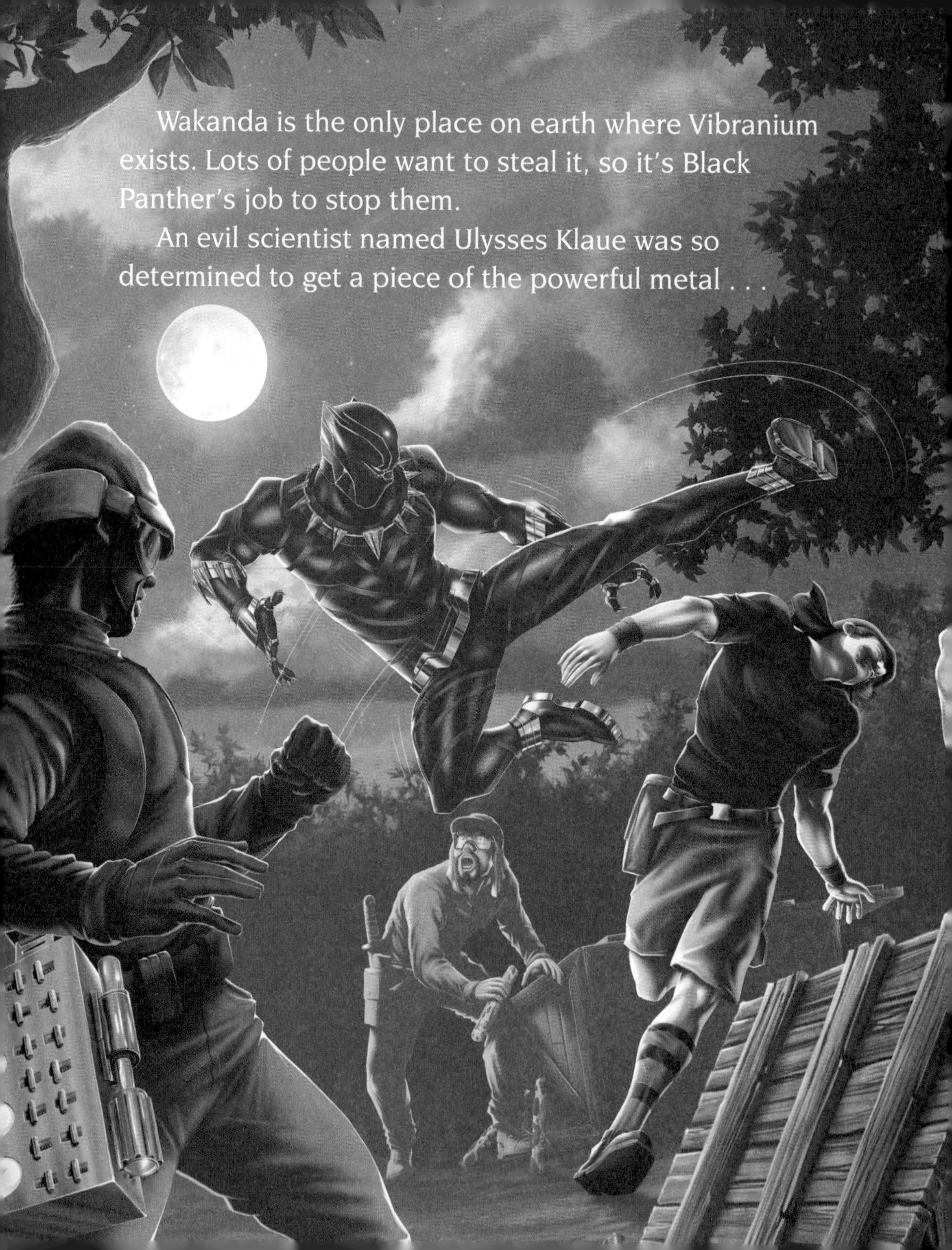

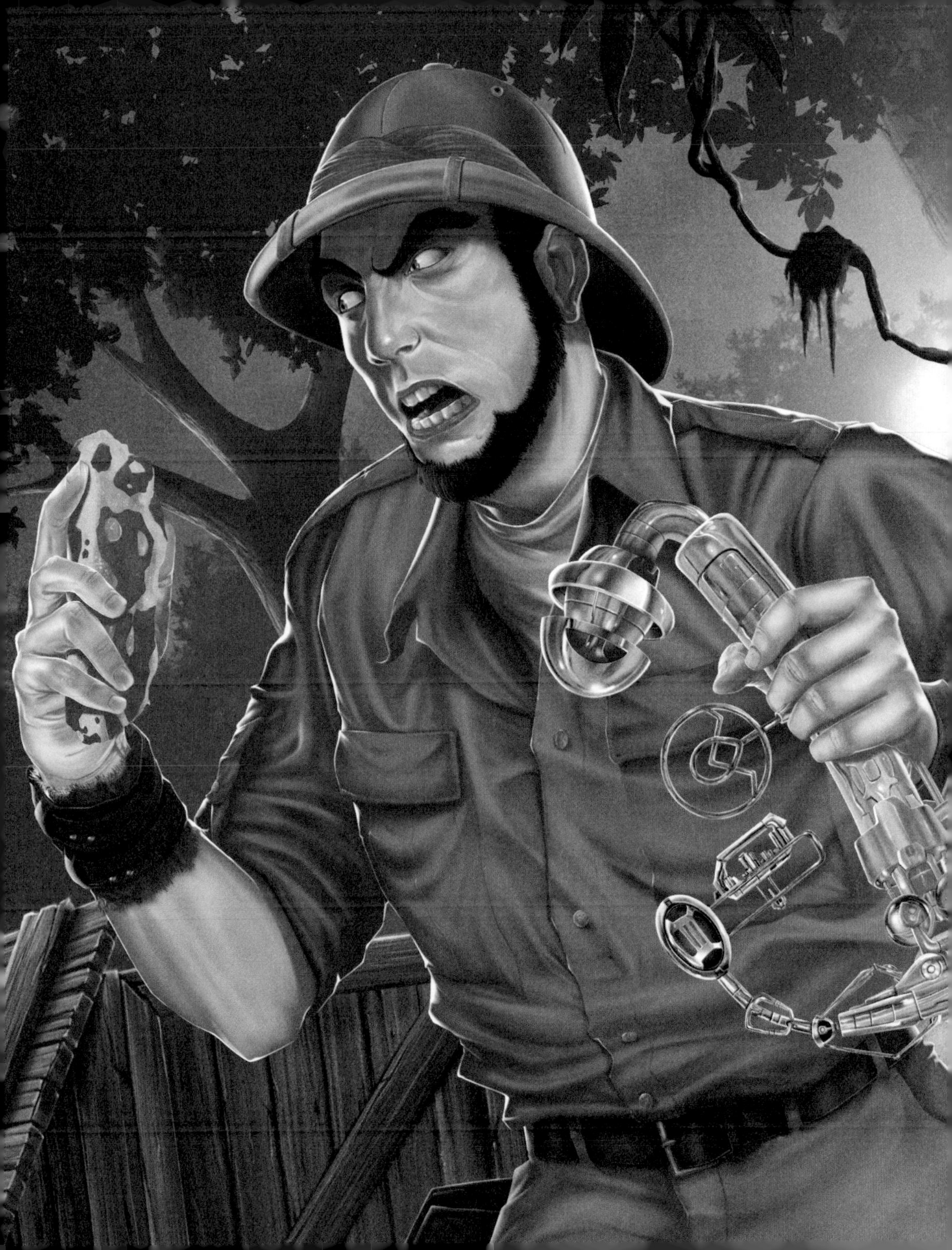

. . . that he became the evil Super Villain known as **KLAW**.

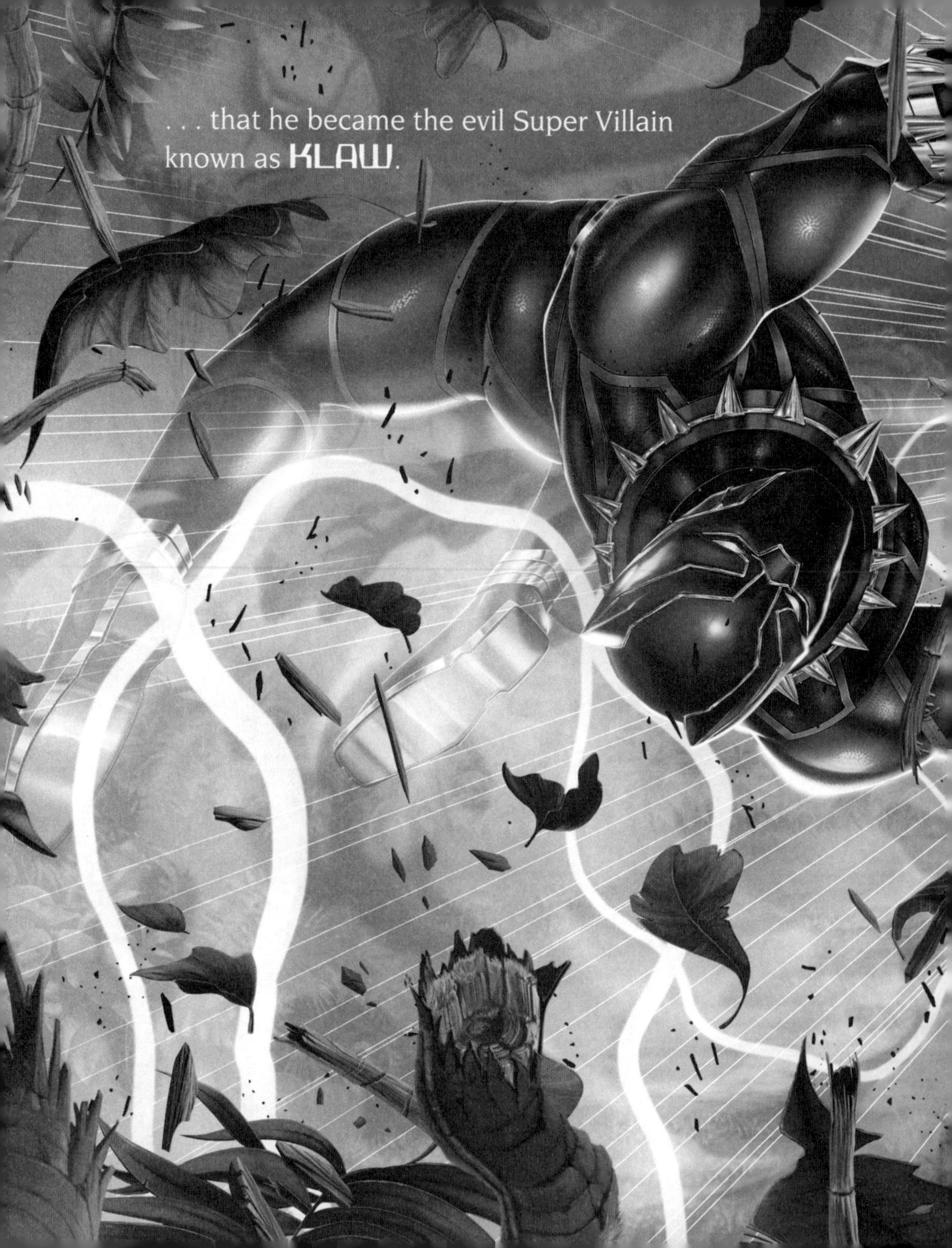

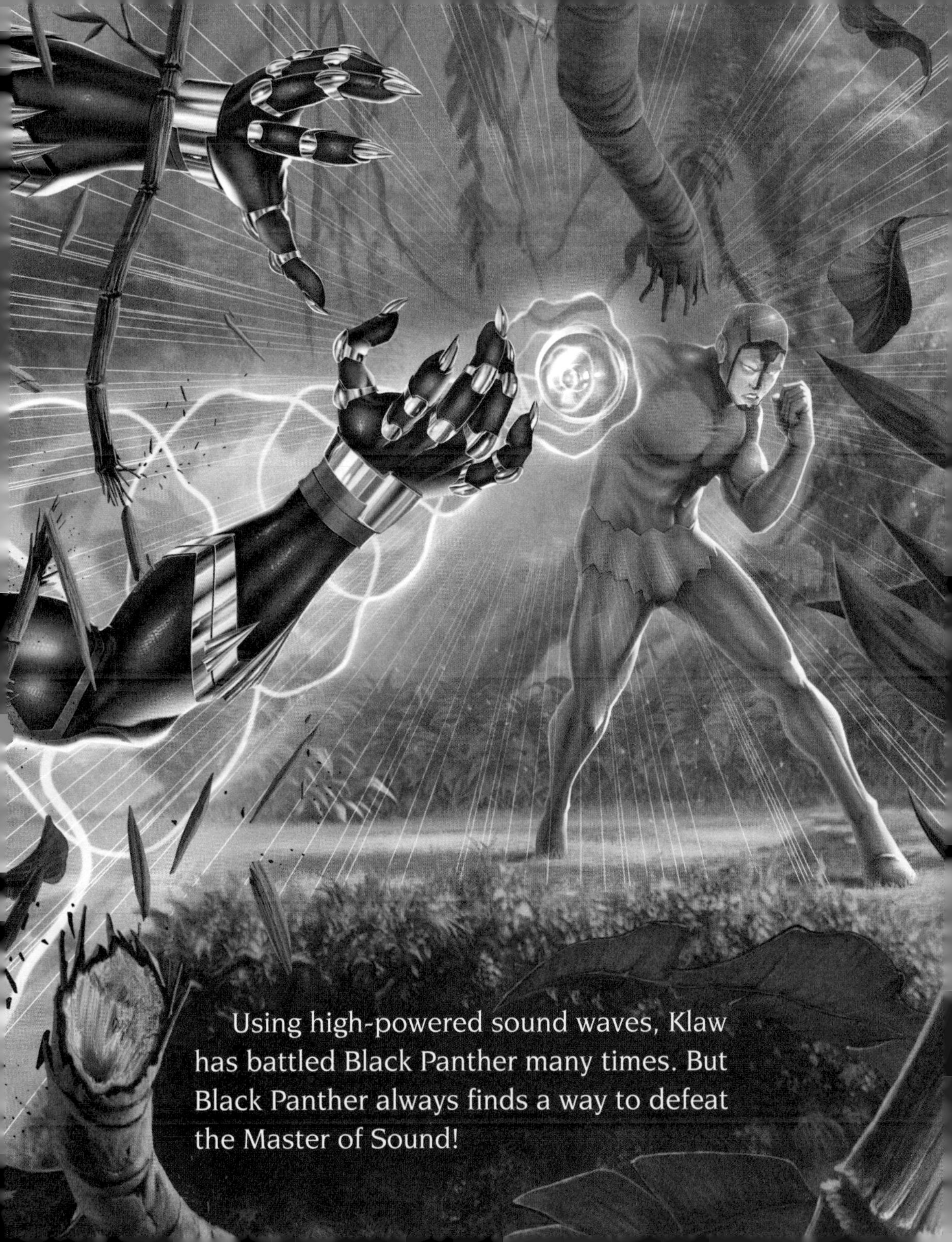

Using high-powered sound waves, Klaw has battled Black Panther many times. But Black Panther always finds a way to defeat the Master of Sound!

Black Panther uses his many incredible powers to fight other villains, such as **MAN-APE**, a human with the strength of a giant gorilla, and . . .

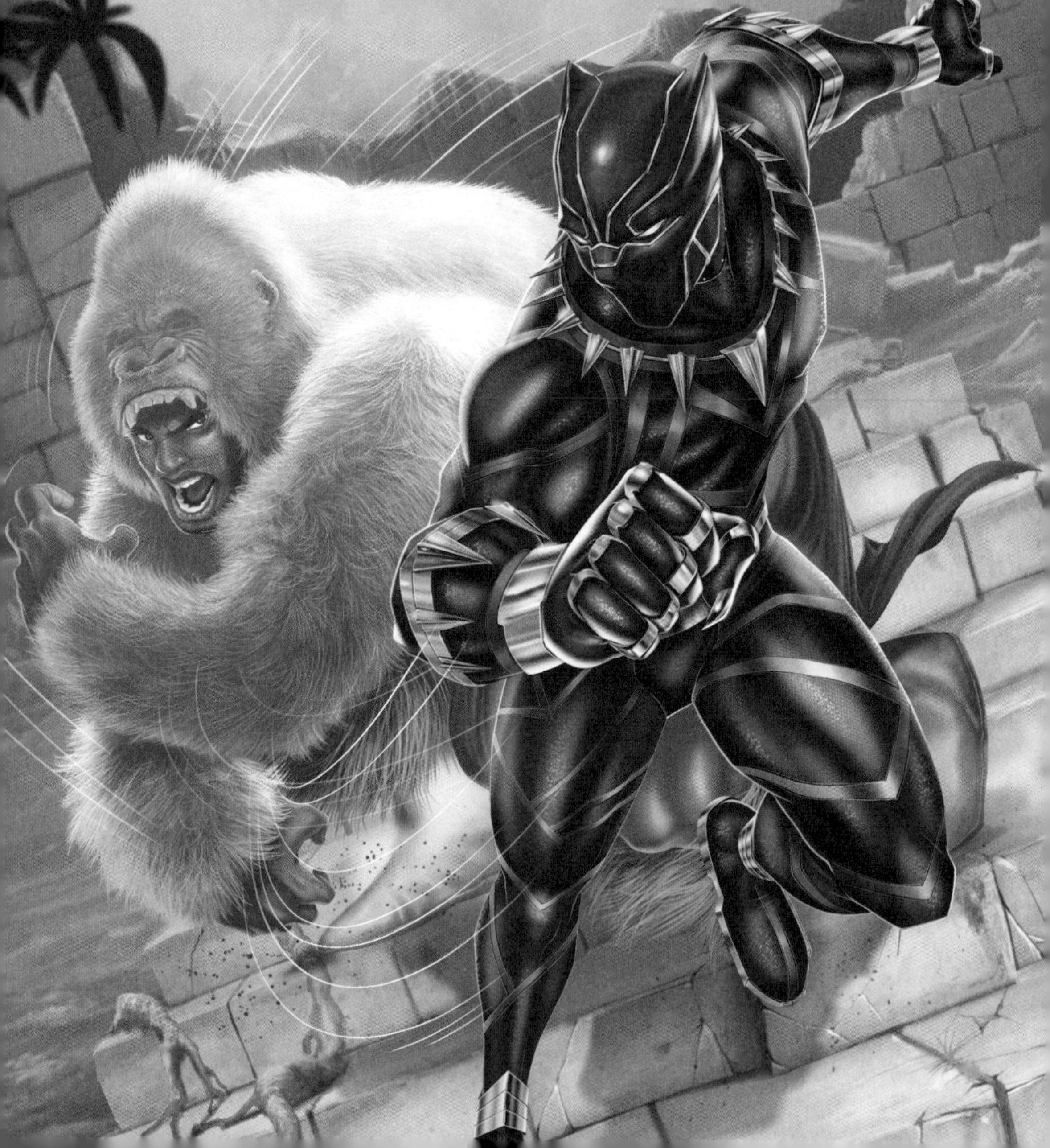

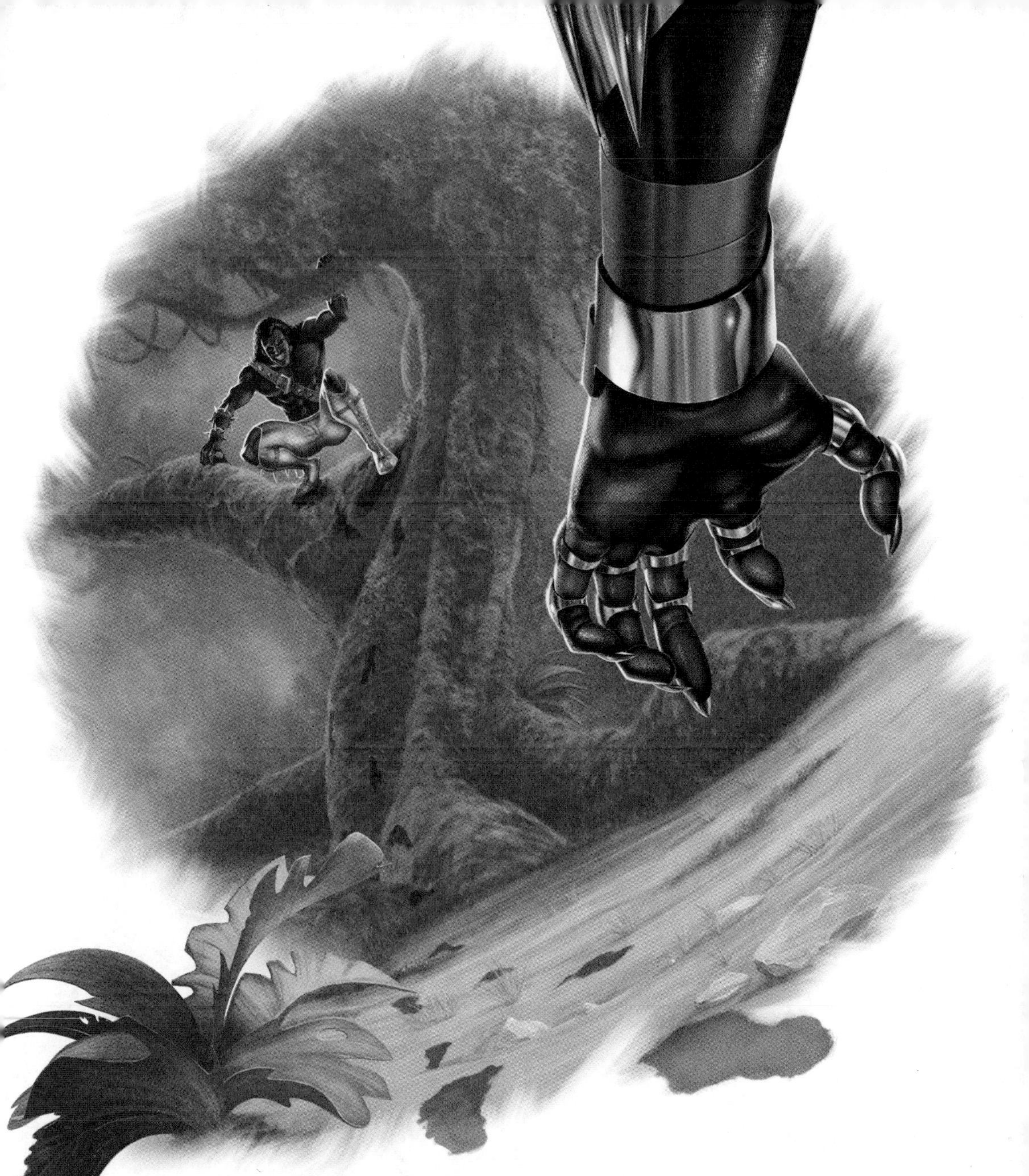

. . . **ERIK KILLMONGER**, a skilled fighter and sworn enemy of Black Panther.

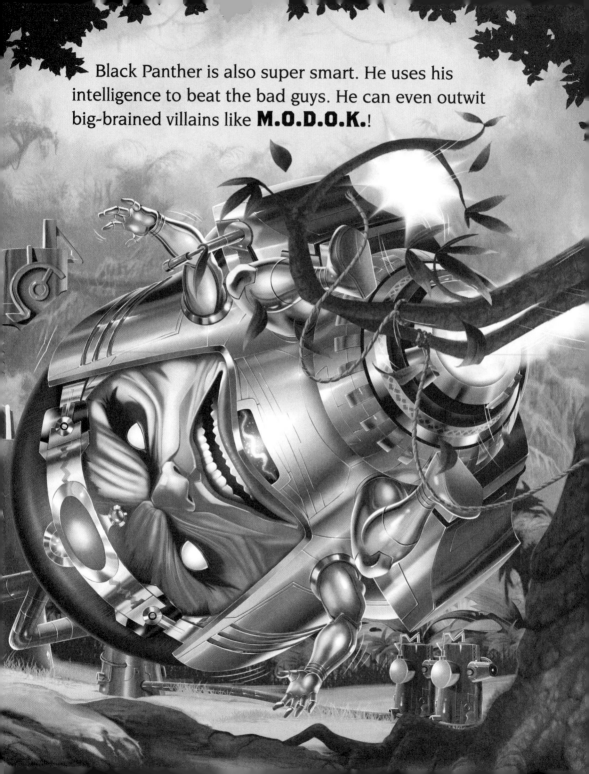

Black Panther is also super smart. He uses his intelligence to beat the bad guys. He can even outwit big-brained villains like **M.O.D.O.K.**!

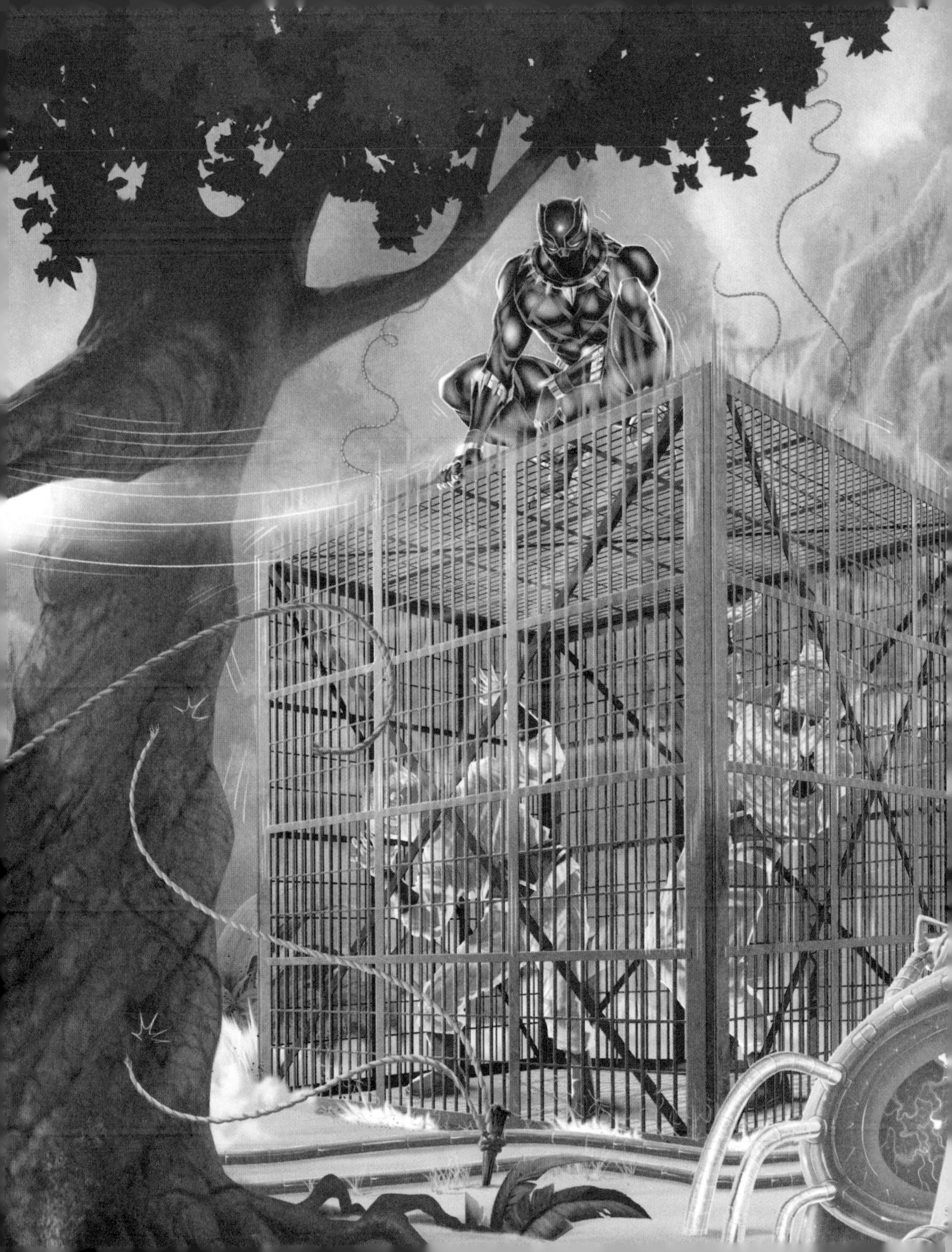

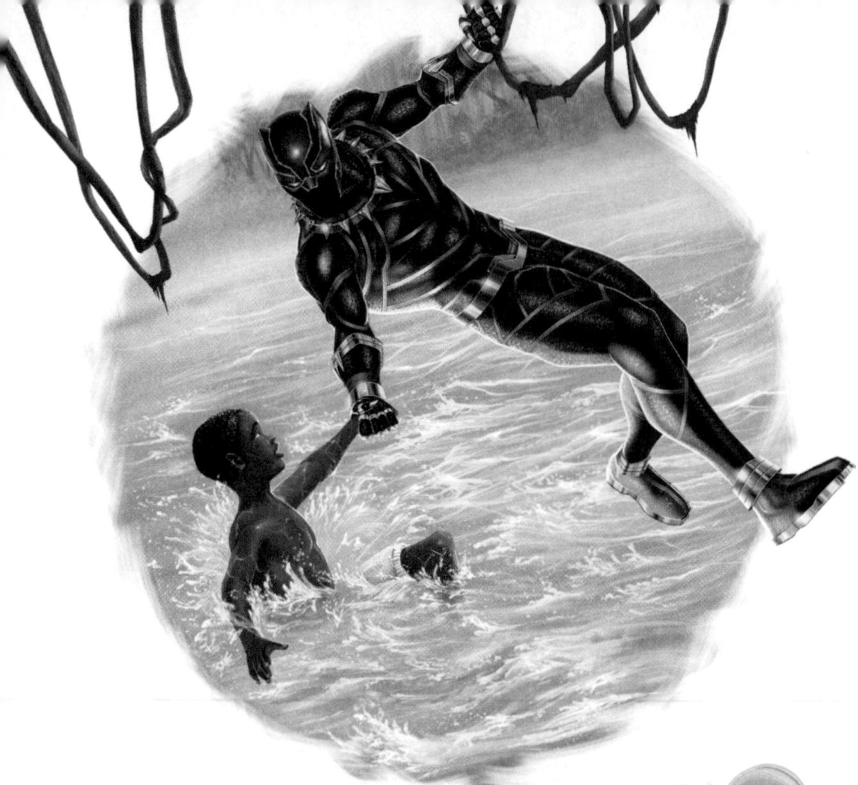

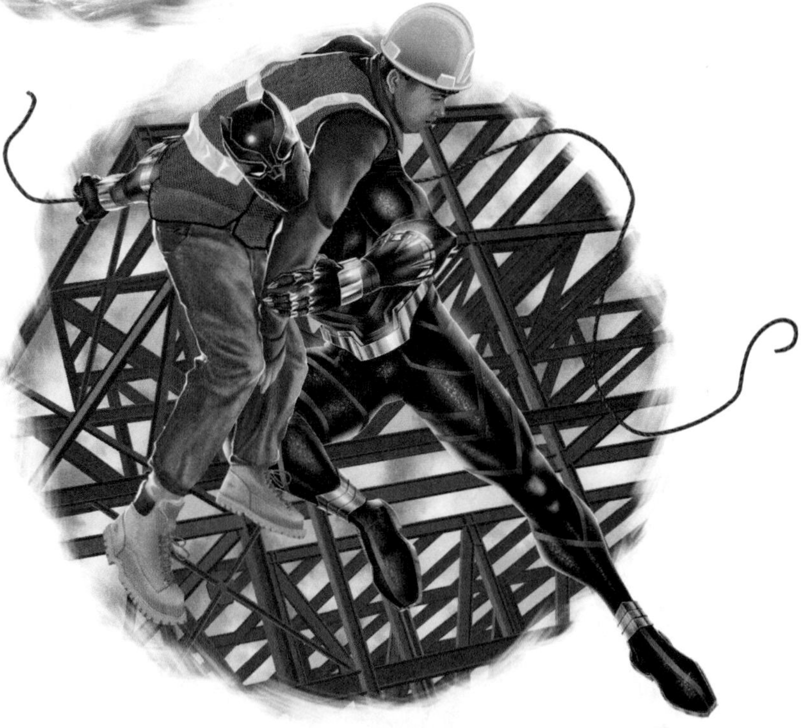

Black Panther is **BRAVE**. When disaster strikes, he always answers the call for help.

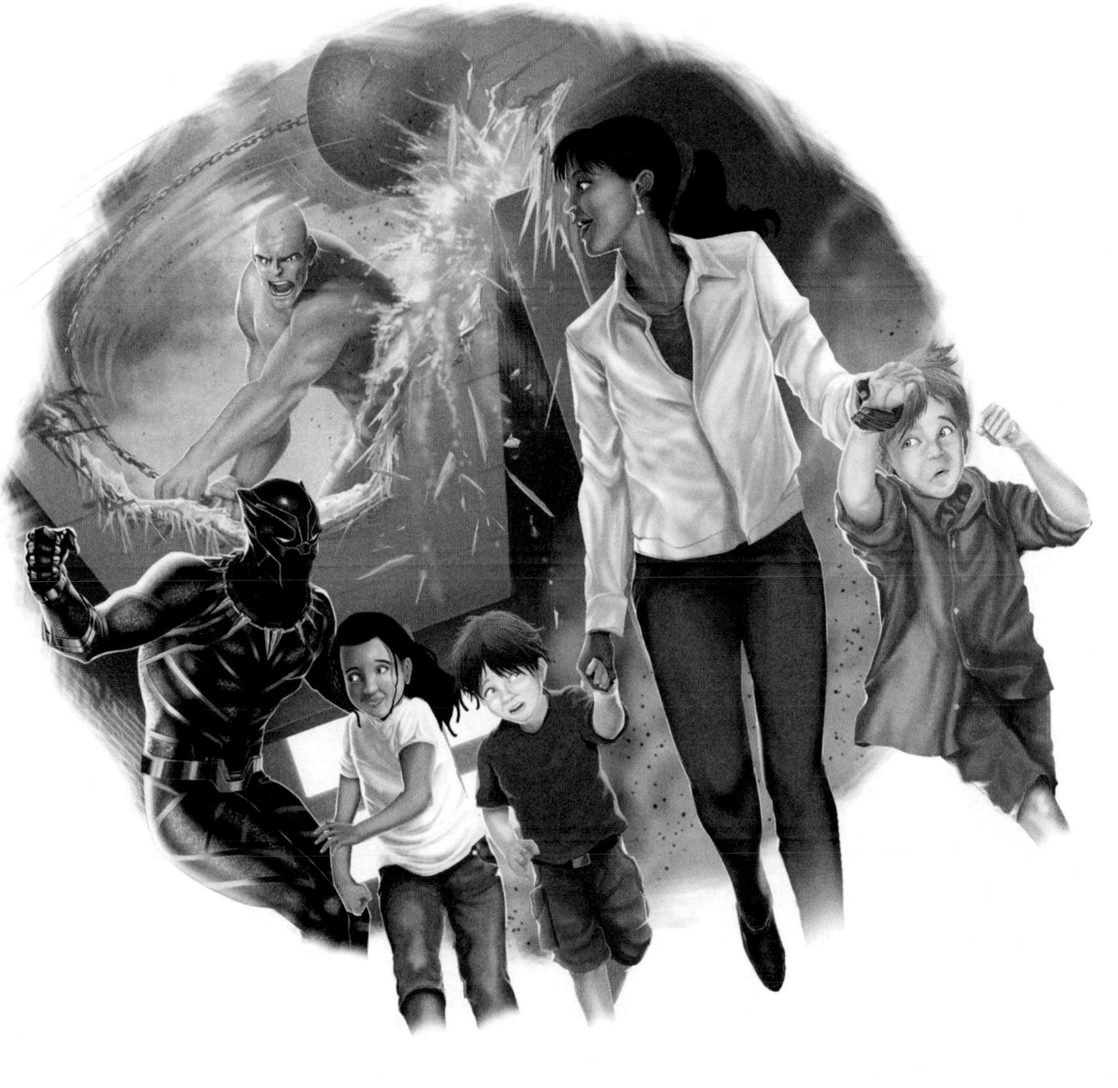

Black Panther has some amazing friends: Black Widow, Thor, Hawkeye, Hulk, Captain America, Iron Man, Wasp, and Ant-Man. Together they are the **AVENGERS**. They battle foes that are too powerful for any one of them to face alone.

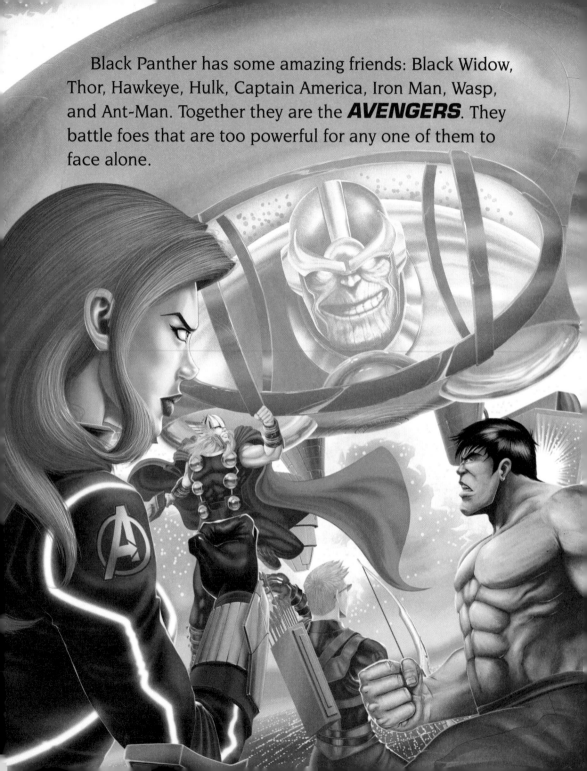

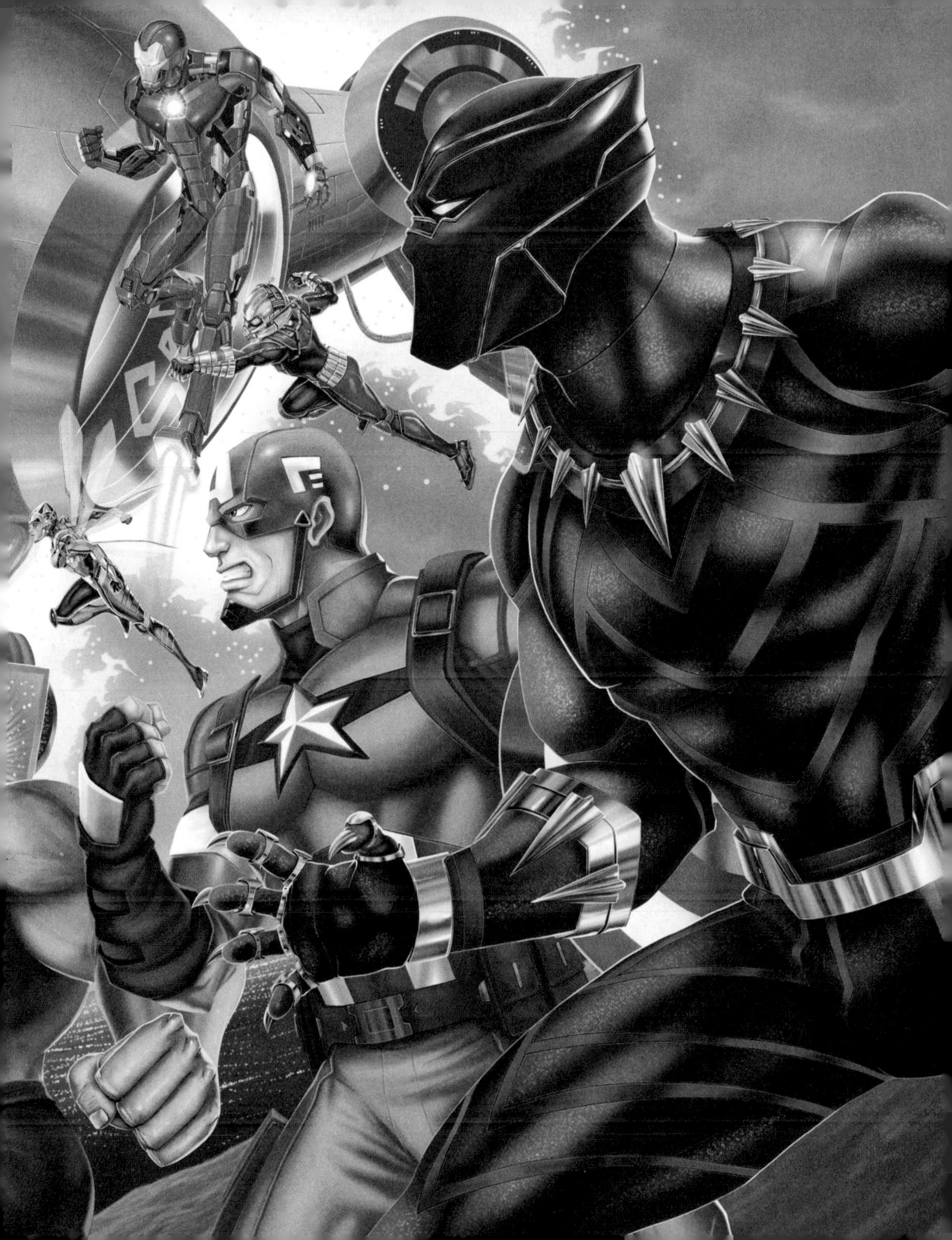

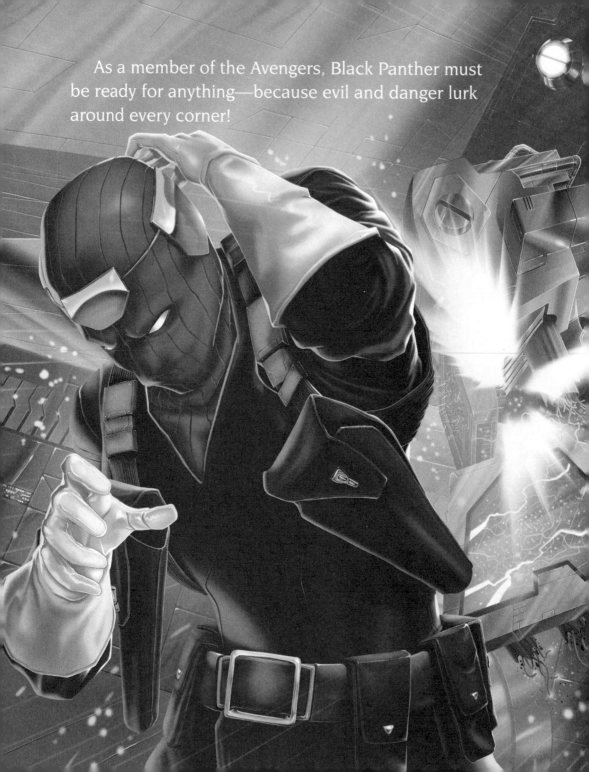

As a member of the Avengers, Black Panther must be ready for anything—because evil and danger lurk around every corner!

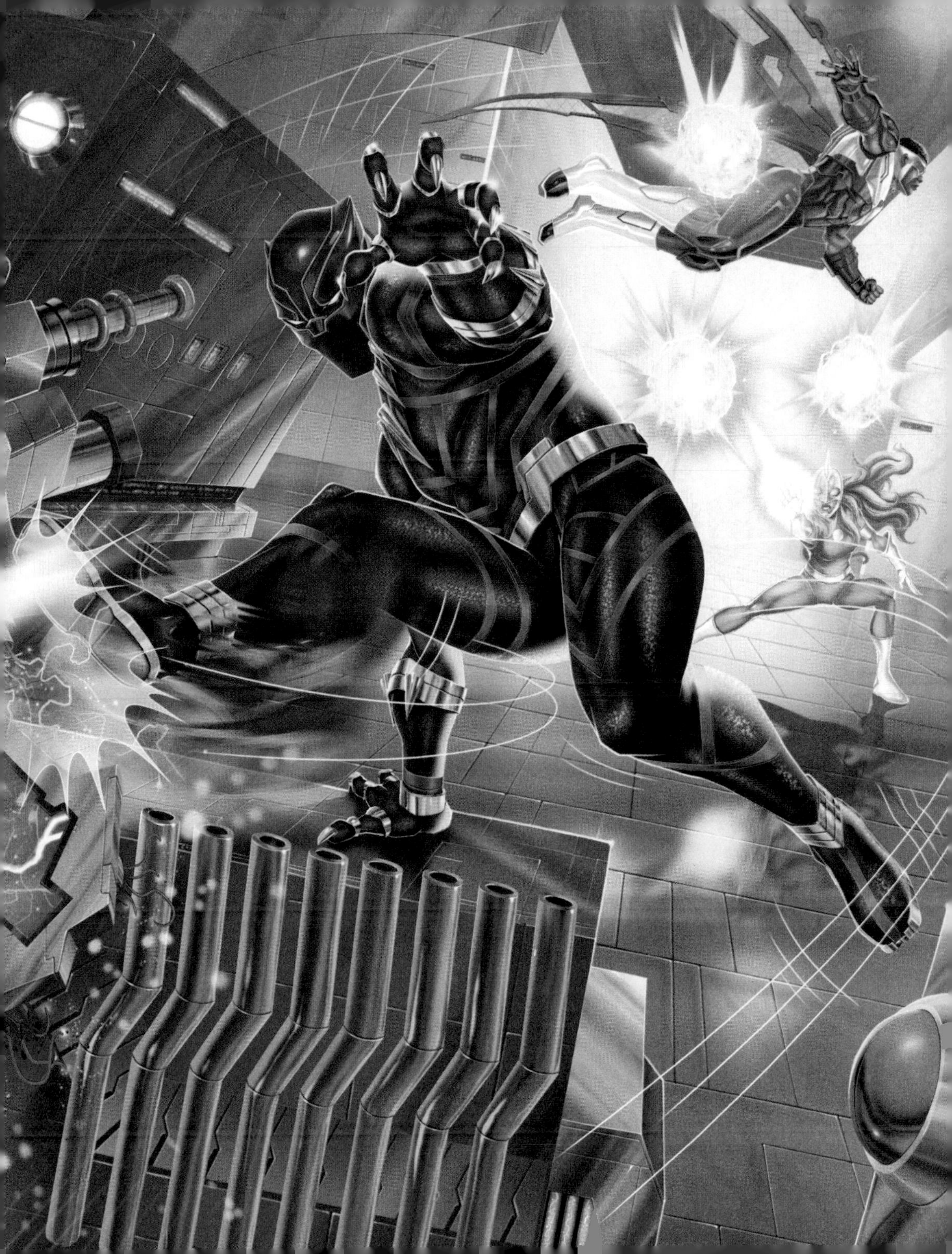

But there's no need to fear when the mighty hero Black Panther is near.

GO, BLACK PANTHER!

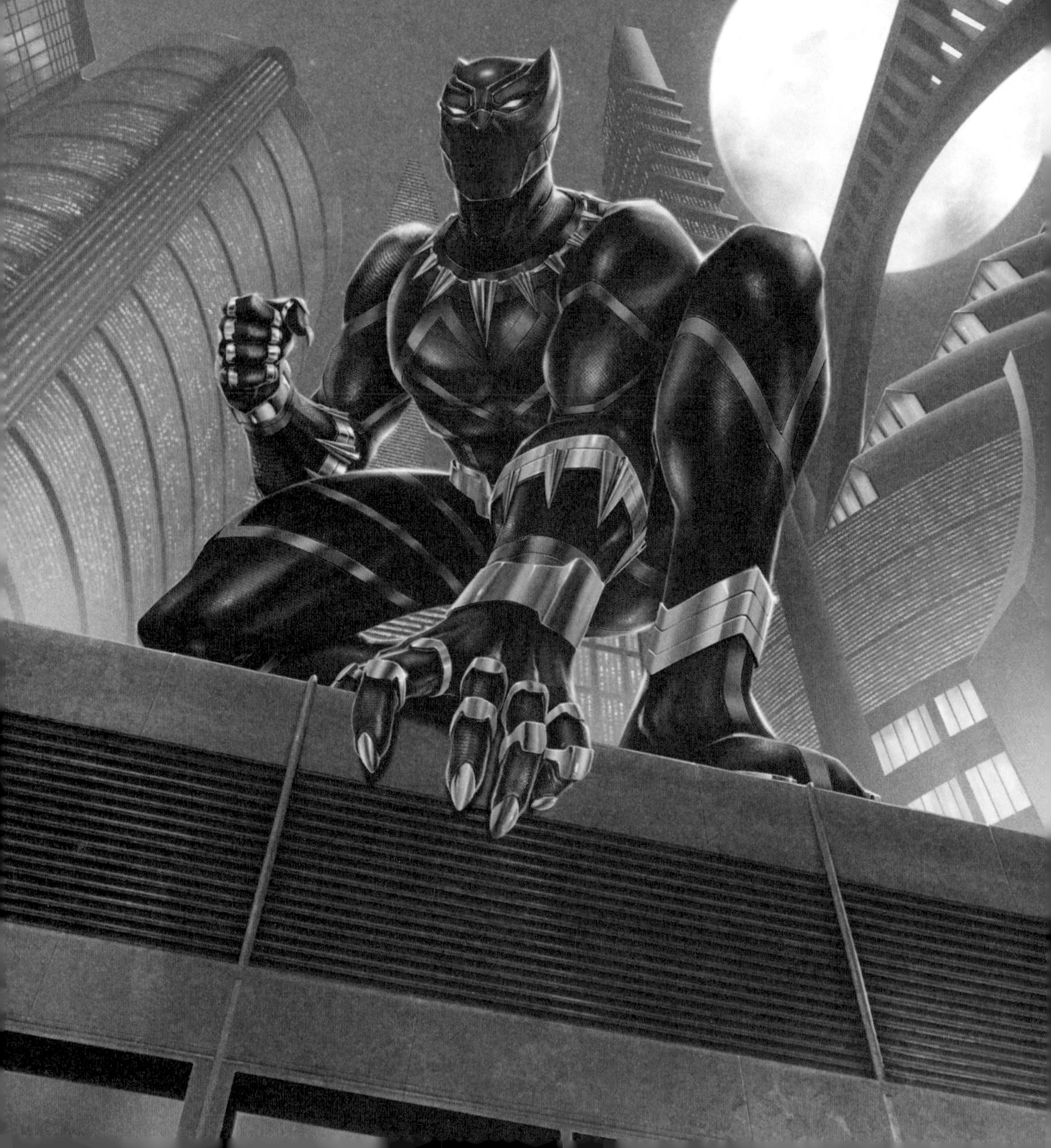